Once upon
a northern
night

ONCE UPON a northern night
while you lay sleeping,
wrapped in a downy blanket,
I painted you a picture.

It started with one tiny flake,
perfect
and beautiful
and special,
just like you.
Then there were two,
and then three.

Soon
the night sky filled with
sparkling specks of white,
crowding
and floating,
tumbling down to the welcoming
ground
until the earth was
wrapped in a downy blanket,
just like you.

Once upon a northern night
pine trees held out prickly hands
to catch the falling flakes
that gathered into puffs of creamy white,
settling like balls of cotton,
waiting.

When you walk beneath the trees
the wind will tickle them
until they drop their snowy treasures,
dusting your hair and
sprinkling your nose.

Once upon a northern night
a mother deer led her fawn
around the silent birch
and traced
a wandering path
on my canvas of white.

They nuzzled the sleeping garden
with memories of summer,
then wandered off
to taste the frozen fruit
still clinging to an apple tree.

Once upon a northern night
a great grey owl gazed down
with his great yellow eyes
on the milky-white bowl of your yard.

Without a sound,
not even the quietest whisper,
his great silent wings lifted and
down,
down,
down
he drifted,
leaving a feathery sketch
of his passing
in the snow.

Once upon a northern night
two snowshoe hares
scampered and chased
as they played a nighttime game of tag.

The fox,
in his auburn coat and long black boots,
wanted to play, too.
But the hares became silent
and oh so still,
crouched beneath the winter-bare dogwood,
playing hide-and-seek
until the fox gave up
and pranced off into the darkness.

Once upon a northern night
a small,
small mouse
with big,
big ears
scurried along the deck,
searching.

Across the table,
mounded with snowy white
like vanilla ice cream,
he ran,
tunnelling beneath the drifts
to a midnight feast of seeds
that lay scattered
beneath the bird feeder.

Once upon a northern night,
deep,
deep
in the darkest hours,
the snowy clouds crept away
and stars appeared –
twinkling points of light
hanging in the purple sky.

I knew by the time you woke,
the sun would have chased them away,
so I set them like diamonds
on the branches of the willow.

Once upon a northern night
melodies of
green and
pink and
orange
sang across the sky.

I tried to capture them
but they were much too nimble,
and only their rhythm reached you,
deep in slumber,
rising and falling
with each sweet,
peaceful breath.

Once upon a northern night
I sent the frost
to dance on your window
and make a frame.

It twirled and twisted,
curled and coiled,
spiralled and spun,
climbing around the edges of the glass
but leaving the middle
as smooth and clear as the frozen pond.

Once upon a northern night
while you lay sleeping,
wrapped in a downy blanket,
I painted you a picture.

And then
I had the moon gently kiss you
and the wind whisper ...

I love you.

To Josiah, Katy and Alex, in loving
memory of their mother, my beautiful
sister, Theresa. – JEP

To J & M
Thank you for your inspiration
and generosity. – IA

Published in the UK in 2015 by Walker Books Ltd
87 Vauxhall Walk, London SE11 5HJ
First published in Canada and the USA in 2013
by Groundwood Books

2 4 6 8 10 9 7 5 3 1

Text © 2013 Jean E. Pendziwol
Illustrations © 2013 Isabelle Arsenault
The right of Jean E. Pendziwol and Isabelle Arsenault to be
identified as the author and illustrator of this work has been
asserted by them in accordance with the Copyright,
Designs and Patents Act 1988

Printed and bound in Malaysia

British Library Cataloguing in Publication Data:
a catalogue record for this book is available from the British Library

ISBN 978-1-4063-6245-9

www.walker.co.uk

FSC
www.fsc.org
MIX
Paper from
responsible sources
FSC® C012700